First American edition published in 2011 by Gecko Press USA, an imprint of Gecko Press Ltd.

Reprinted 2012

A catalog record for this book is available from the US Library of Congress.

Distributed in the United States and Canada by
Lerner Publishing Group, Inc.
241 First Avenue North
Minneapolis, MN 55401 USA
www.lernerbooks.com

This translation first published in New Zealand and Australia in 2007 by Gecko Press
PO Box 9335, Marion Square, Wellington 6141, New Zealand
Email: info@geckopress.com

Original title: *C'est moi le plus fort*
Text and illustrations © 2006 *l'école des loisirs*, Paris

English translation © Gecko Press 2007

Translator: Jean Anderson
Typesetting: Archetype, Wellington, New Zealand
Printing: Everbest, China

ISBN Hardback 978-0-9582787-7-5

For more curiously good books, visit www.geckopress.com

Mario Ramos

I am so STRONG

GECKO PRESS

One day, after a fine and filling meal, the wolf decided to go for a walk in the woods.

"Just the thing for the digestion," he said. "And while I'm at it, I'll find out what everyone thinks of me."

First he came across a very small rabbit.

"Hello there, Sugar Bun," he said. "Tell me, who do you think is the strongest around here?"

"Oh, you are, Mister Wolf. Absolutely, definitely, no doubt about it!" replied the rabbit.

Pleased as punch, the wolf went on
through the woods.

"Oh, it's so good to be me!" he said, breathing
in the scents of oak and mushroom.

Next he came upon Little Red Riding Hood.

"My dear, how well that crimson suits you. You look sweet enough to eat. Tell me, my little strawberry, who's the strongest in the woods?"

"Oh, you are, absolutely. Yes, you, Mister Wolf. There's no question," she answered. "You're the strongest in the woods!"

"Ha! Just as I thought—I'm the strongest.
It doesn't matter how often I'm told.
One can never have too many compliments,"
said the wolf.

Then he met the three little pigs.

"Hello, what have we here? Three little pigs, a long way from home. That's a bit careless. Tell me, little bacon bits, who's the strongest in the woods?"

"The strongest, the toughest, the handsomest— that's you of course, Big Bad Wolf!" the piglets cried together.

"Everyone knows!
I'm the fiercest and the cruelest!
I *am* the Big Bad Wolf. They're all
scared to death of me. I'm the king!" the
wolf trumpeted at the top of his voice.

A little further on, he came upon the seven dwarves.

"Heigh-ho, you hard-working little chaps!
Do you know who's the strongest in the woods?"
he asked.

"The strongest? That's you, Mister Wolf," the little
men said all together.

"Aha! That settles it! There's no contest.
Everyone agrees. I'm the terror of the woods,
the baddest guy around!" howled the wolf.

Next he came upon a little toad of some sort.

"Hello, horrid thing. I suppose *you* know who's the strongest in the woods?" asked the wolf.

"Of course I do. It's my mother," replied the little toad of some sort.

"What?! You pathetic little gargoyle!
Miserable gizzard! Gumboil! Tell me again.
I can't have heard you properly.
Who is the strongest?"

"I told you. My mother's the strongest and also the kindest. Unless someone's giving me a hard time," replied the baby dragon. "Who are you?"

"Who me? Oh, me... I'm just a harmless little wolf," said the wolf, backing prudently away.

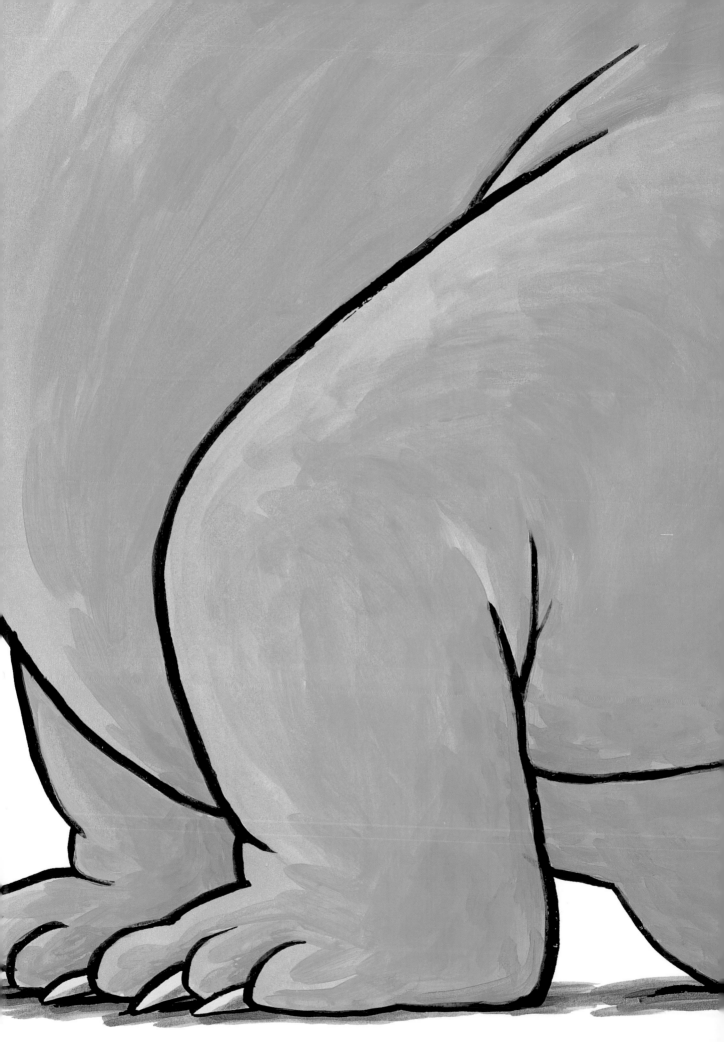